Mrs. Wigglesworth's Hat

Written by:

Pat Erickson

Illustrated by:

Michael McMullin &
Sue Brown

For Steve – who believes in me even when I don't believe in myself.

For Lindsey, Jesse, Jacob and Stella who made reading to them so much fun that I wanted to share the gift of reading with other children.

Thank you, thank you, thank you to Sue & Michael; this wouldn't have happened without you two.

P.E.

In Memory of my beloved Alice

M.McM.

 For my big sister Pat – for showing me that it is impossible to be defeated when you have a spirit as courageous as hers and who has always believed that I can do anything that she puts her mind to. Vintage fashion or modern vogue whichever hat you wear Pat, you wear it well.

And for JC, JB & Pops, my source, inspiration and support

S.B.

For - Alice who would be so proud!

All

Printed in the United States of America

First printing 2015

ISBN 978-1-48356-099-1

Book Baby Publishing

bookbaby.com

MRS. WIGGLESWORTH'S HAT

Written by PAT ERICKSON

Illustrated by Michael McMullin & Sue Brown

Mrs. Wigglesworth is a lady who loves to tell stories to children.

Once a week, she gets all dressed up, puts on one of her nicest hats and goes to school to tell stories.

One day, Mrs. Wigglesworth was visiting at Meridian Park School. She loves visiting at Meridian Park School and especially loves telling stories to kindergarten students.

As she was walking from her car into the school, a gust of wind came up. The wind blew Mrs. Wigglesworth's hat right off her head.

Mrs. Wigglesworth tried to chase it, but she wasn't as young as she used to be. She couldn't run as fast as she did when she was younger.

Each time she was almost within reach of the hat, the wind would pick it up again and carry it farther away. At last, the wind took the hat and blew it out of sight. The hat was gone.

Mrs. Wigglesworth didn't know what to do. She always wore a hat when she told stories. She didn't have time to go home and get another hat. Without a hat, would the children even know who she was?

She looked through her car and didn't see another hat. She did see her umbrella. "Well, at least that's something", she said to herself. She put the umbrella on her head and started to walk into the school building. Fortunately it was a collapsible umbrella with a short handle.

Once she got in the building, Mrs. Wigglesworth went to the office. She needed to tell Roxie, the school secretary, that she was visiting today. Roxie looked up from her work and said, "Mrs. Wigglesworth, whatever is on your head?"

Mrs. Wigglesworth explained all about the wind stealing her hat, and how without a hat, she was worried the children might not recognize her. So, she was using the umbrella as a hat.

Roxie listened, and then said, "Mrs. Wigglesworth, your umbrella doesn't make a very good hat - all those metal pieces are poking you. Here, we can make a hat from a newspaper. I have one on my desk that I've finished reading. We can use it."

Roxie showed Mrs. Wigglesworth how to fold a newspaper in order to make a hat. Mrs. Wigglesworth put the newspaper hat on her head.

"Thank you, Roxie," she said. "This does make me feel more like myself." She started to walk down the hallway to the kindergarten classrooms.

Along the way, Mrs. Wigglesworth ran into Mr. Mike, who worked in the school library helping children find books they loved to read.

"Why Mrs. Wigglesworth, what kind of hat is that?" asked Mr. Mike.

Mrs. Wigglesworth explained all about the wind stealing her hat, about using her umbrella for a hat and how Roxie helped her make this hat.

"That was very nice of Roxie, but a paper hat might rip and it really doesn't look like your hats." Mr. Mike took a hat from a rack near his office door. It was a baseball cap. "Wear this cap, Mrs. Wigglesworth. It's one of my favorite caps. It's a nice bright color like your hats, but it won't tear like a paper hat."

Mrs. Wigglesworth put on the baseball cap, thanked Mr. Mike, and continued toward the kindergarten classrooms. Now that she didn't have to worry so much about ripping the hat, she felt much more like herself.

Mrs. Wigglesworth passed the school nurse's office. The nurse Mrs. Allred, called out, "Mrs. Wigglesworth, why are you wearing a baseball cap? Are you going to a game?"

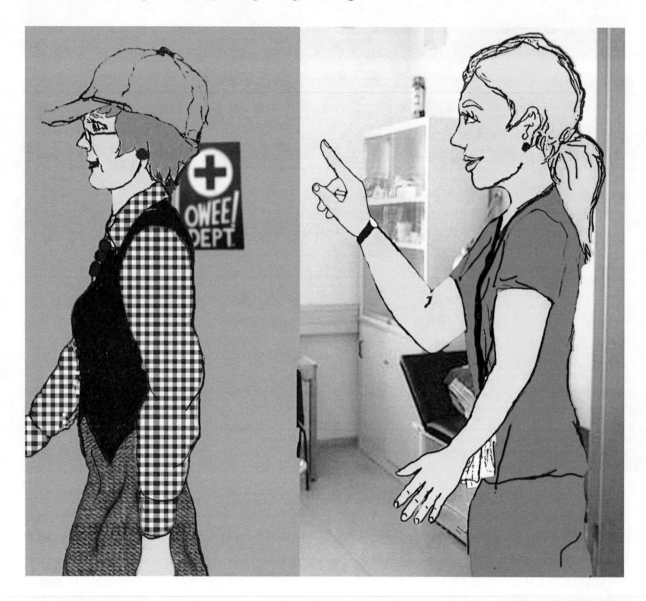

Mrs. Wigglesworth explained all about the wind stealing her hat, about the umbrella hat, the newspaper hat, and how Mr. Mike had just given her the baseball cap.

The nurse agreed, "It is a nice baseball cap, but it just doesn't look like your hats, Mrs. Wigglesworth." She reached into her cabinet and pulled out a little white hat. "We nurses used to wear these types of hats, but not anymore. Perhaps it will look nice on you.

Mrs. Wigglesworth agreed this was a very nice hat, and she put the little white hat on her head. Then she thanked the nurse and continued through the hallway toward kindergarten. The nurse's hat made Mrs. Wigglesworth feel even more like herself.

Along the way, she passed by Ms. Phelan's fourth grade classroom. Ms. Phelan called out to her, "Mrs. Wigglesworth, are you a nurse?"

"Oh no", said Mrs. Wigglesworth and she explained all about the wind stealing her hat, about the umbrella hat, the newspaper hat, the baseball cap and how the school nurse had just given her the white nurses' hat.

"It is a nice hat," Ms. Phelan agreed, "but it just doesn't look like your hats." She went into her classroom and took out a box of hats that her students used when they performed plays.

"Hmmmm," said Ms Phelan as she sorted through the hats. "Maybe this one will do." Ms. Phelan pulled from the box a prarie hat - the sort of hat pioneer women wore. It was made from a pink flowered fabric. "At least this hat has flowers on it", Ms. Phelan pointed out.

Mrs. Wigglesworth agreed that the flowered fabric was quite pretty and she put the hat on her head. The flowers made Mrs. Wigglesworth smile. She felt almost like herself. After thanking Ms. Phelan, she continued on her way.

When Mrs. Wigglesworth finally arrived at the kindergarten classrooms, she found Mr. Herold, one of the teachers, out in the hallway. Mr. Herold looked at Mrs. Wigglesworth and her hat. He said, "Mrs. Wigglesworth what an unusual hat you are wearing today."

Mrs. Wigglesworth explained all about the wind stealing her hat, about the umbrella hat, the newspaper hat, the baseball cap, the nurse's hat and how Ms. Phelan had just given her this hat.

Mr. Herold said, "That's a fine hat, but it just doesn't look like your hats." Mr. Herold disappeared into his classroom and came back a few moments later with a big pink floppy hat with flowers all over it. This looked very much like Mrs. Wigglesworth's own hats.

"Here Mrs. Wigglesworth," said Mr. Herold. "I borrowed this hat from our class dress-up box. This looks more like your hats."

Mrs. Wigglesworth agreed and put the pink floppy hat on her head. Now she looked and felt just like herself. Mrs. Wigglesworth was ready to tell stories.

She followed Mr. Herold into the classroom where she told three stories to the kindergarten children. When she had finished, she gave the pink floppy hat back to Mr. Herold so that his students could still use it for dress up.

Mrs. Wigglesworth thought about her morning. She felt thankful. Her good friends made sure she didn't have to tell stories without a hat. She was quite happy. As she walked down the hall, Mrs. Wigglesworth was humming to herself. She wasn't paying attention to where she was going, and nearly bumped into a group of students on their way to the library.

The children's voices rang out with greetings.
"Hi Mrs. W."
"Hello, Mrs. Wigglesworth."
"Mrs. Wigglesworth, where is your hat?"

Mrs. Wigglesworth practically burst with happiness. Why? Because now she knew the children DID recognize her even when she wasn't wearing a hat. She could tell stories whether she wore a hat or not. She said goodbye to the students and went on her way.

From that time on, sometimes Mrs. Wigglesworth wore a hat to tell stories and sometimes she didn't. However, whenever she wore a hat on a windy day, she always remembered to put one hand firmly on her head.

THE
END

Make a Paper Hat just like Mrs. Wigglesworth!

You can make a newspaper hat just like Roxie and Mrs. Wigglesworth made. Turn the page for step by step instructions.

Make your own Paper Hat!

STEP 1.

Fold newspaper in half

(Like it comes)

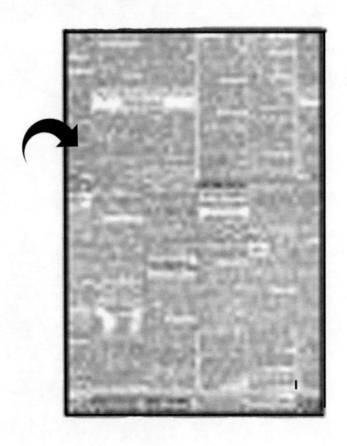

STEP 2.
Fold top down to meet bottom

STEP 3.

Fold right and left sides towards the middle to form a point

STEP 4.

Open bottom, and fold bottom up on back and front

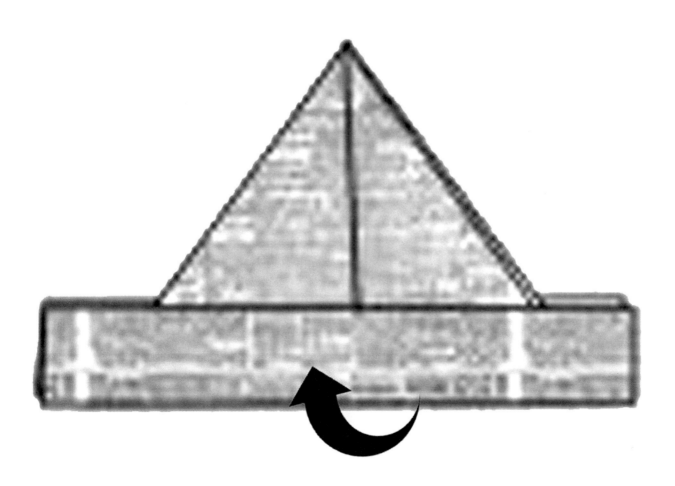

STEP 5.
Wear!